THE ADVENTURES OF WISE OLD OWL

by ROBERT KRAUS

Troll Associates

4
PARKER PELICAN + PAM PARROT

Printed in the United States of America

1   3   5   7   9   10   8   6   4   2

Library of Congress Cataloging in Publication Data

Kraus, Robert, (date)
    The adventures of Wise Old Owl / written and illustrated by Robert
Kraus.
       p.   cm
    Summary: Wise Old Owl, the author, takes time out from his work to
visit a class of aspiring young writers.
    ISBN 0-8167-2943-3 (lib. bdg.)   ISBN 0-8167-2944-1 (pbk.)
    [1. Authors—Fiction. 2. Owls—Fiction. 3. Animals—Fiction.]
I. Title.
PZ7.K868Ad   1993
[E]—dc20
                                   92-20436

Wise Old Owl, beloved author, lived and worked in a hollow tree, deep in the heart of the Magic Forest.

Every morning, after a quick birdbath, he had a bowl of birdseed and milk, and a cup of steaming hot chocolate. Mmm. Mmm, good.

Then he sat at his typewriter and typed up
one of his enchanting stories. Before he knew it,
it was time for lunch.

He took a short walk through the Magic Forest, to the Birdcage Cafe, where he ate some bread crumbs and gravy. Mmm. Mmm, good.

Then it was back to the hollow tree to paint illustrations for his stories. He tried not to get any paint on his feathers while he worked—it was the dickens to get off.

Wise Old Owl was pleased with his pictures,
but he was also tired. He decided to take a nap.
Tomorrow was going to be a very busy day.

Wise Old Owl got up at the crack of dawn, took a birdbath, and ate a birdseed cookie. Then he hopped into his red roadster and tootled through the woods on his way to Miss Bear's class in the Little Schoolhouse in the Pines. He was looking forward to meeting her class and awarding a prize to the best book by a young animal author.

When he arrived, Wise Old Owl was pleased to see a big sign that said, WELCOME, WISE OLD OWL. The animal students danced around him, and whispered to each other.

"That's Wise Old Owl," said Pearl Squirrel.

"How can you tell?" asked Chip Chipmunk.

"Well, he looks like a *wise old owl*," said Pearl.

"May I have your autograph, sir?" asked a little mouse.

"Of course," answered Wise Old Owl.

Miss Bear gave Wise Old Owl a big bear hug.
"I just love your books," she said. "Do come in
and have some bread and honey."

14

"Thank you kindly," said Wise Old Owl. He ate the bread and honey carefully. Honey was the dickens to get out of feathers.

"Boys and girls," said Miss Bear, "it is a pleasure to introduce Wise Old Owl, beloved author. Let's make him feel welcome."

All the students clapped their paws and wings together.

"Hoot, hoot," said Wise Old Owl. "I am happy to be here today to tell you about my books, and to award the WISE OLD OWL MEDAL to the best book written by you, the young authors."

Wise Old Owl began his talk by drawing
pictures of his favorite characters.

"How do you get your ideas?" asked Pearl Squirrel.

"Ideas are all around us, if we open our eyes," said Wise Old Owl, opening *his* eyes. "I like to share my ideas with others. That's why I write them down."

All the young authors were busily taking notes.

Then it was time for the contest.

Young Eugene Fieldmouse brought up his book first. "Once, there was a little fieldmouse who visited his cousin in the city. He did not like it, and he went home."

Pearl Squirrel read her book next. "Once there was a squirrel who had a bushy tail. One day she lost her tail. She looked everywhere, but she could not find it."

Chip Chipmunk was last.
"I like chocolate chip cookies.
I like chocolate chip cake.
I ate a box of cookies,
and got a tummyache."

All of the stories were very good. "This is really a problem," said Wise Old Owl. "You are all such talented young authors. Lucky for me, I have three medals in my pocket—one for each of you!"

"Hooray! Hooray! Hooray!" shouted Chip Chipmunk, Pearl Squirrel, and Eugene Fieldmouse. The young authors lined up to receive their medals.

When Chip got his, he gave a little speech in rhyme.

> "I want to thank my mother,
> I want to thank my dad.
> I want to thank this wise old owl,
> He's made me very glad."

Before he left, Wise Old Owl sat down behind a little table and signed copies of all his books. He signed so many that he thought his wing was going to fall off. Then he looked at his watch.

"My goodness," he said. "It is getting late. I must be off."

"Good-bye, Wise Old Owl," said the students.
"Keep up the good work," said Wise Old Owl.
Then he hopped into his little red roadster and
tootled through the woods to the old hollow tree
he called home.

He flopped into his big armchair and loosened his bow tie. He felt happy to be such a beloved author. But, he had no one to tell how many books he had autographed today.

Wise Old Owl changed into his nightshirt and flopped into bed.

The next morning, there was a knocking at the
door.

Knock! Knock! Knock!

Wise Old Owl tumbled out of bed.

"Special delivery," said the mailman.

It was a big envelope filled with fan mail from Miss Bear's class.

He popped back into bed, put on his glasses,
and read each letter twice.

To a writer like Wise Old Owl, being loved by
his fans was sweeter than a beakful of birdseed pie!